NEW YORK REVIEW BOOKS
CLASSICS

SAMSKARA

UDUPI RAJAGOPALACHARYA ANANTHAMURTHY
(1932–2014) was born in the Shimoga district in Karnataka,
India. He studied English literature at the University of Mysore
and received his doctorate from the University of Birmingham,
England. He was a professor of English literature at the
University of Mysore and the author of five novels, three
volumes of poetry, a play, and many collections of short stories
and essays. A socialist, Ananthamurthy was instrumental in the
development of the Navya (or "new") movement in Kannada
literature. In 1995 he received the Jnanpith Award, India's
highest literary honor, and in 2013 he was short-listed for the
Man Booker International Prize.

A. K. RAMANUJAN (1929–1993) was born Attipat Krishna-
swami Ramanujan in Mysore, India, and grew up speaking
Tamil, English, Sanskrit, and Kannada. A poet, translator, and
scholar, for thirty-two years Ramanujan served in both the
Department of Linguistics and the South Asian Languages
and Civilizations Department at the University of Chicago.
His many publications include *The Collected Poems of A. K.
Ramanujan* and *The Collected Essays of A. K. Ramanujan*.

SAMSKARA

A Rite for a Dead Man

U. R. ANANTHAMURTHY

Translated from the Kannada by

A. K. RAMANUJAN

NEW YORK REVIEW BOOKS

New York

THIS IS A NEW YORK REVIEW BOOK
PUBLISHED BY THE NEW YORK REVIEW OF BOOKS
435 Hudson Street, New York, NY 10014
www.nyrb.com

Originally published in English in 1976 by Oxford University Press India and
reprinted here by arrangement with the publisher.

Library of Congress Cataloging-in-Publication Data
Names: Anantha Murthy, U. R., 1932–2014 author. | Ramanujan, A. K.,
   1929–1993 translator.
Title: Samskara : a rite for a dead man / by U. R. Ananthamurthy ; translated
   and with an introduction by A. K. Ramanujan.
Other titles: Saṃskāra. English
Description: New York : New York Review Books, 2016. | Series: New York
   Review Books classics
Identifiers: LCCN 2016019584| ISBN 9781590179123 (alk. paper) | ISBN
   9781590179130 (ebook)
Subjects: LCSH: India—Social life and customs—Fiction. | Funeral rites and
   ceremonies—India—Fiction.
Classification: LCC PL4659.A5 S213 2016 | DDC 894.8/14371—dc23
LC record available at https://lccn.loc.gov/2016019584

ISBN 978-1-59017-912-3
Available as an electronic book; ISBN 978-1-59017-913-0

Printed in the United States of America on acid-free paper.
10 9 8 7 6 5 4 3 2

CONTENTS

TRANSLATOR'S NOTE

U. R. ANANTHAMURTHY's *Samskara* is an important novel of the sixties. It is a religious novella about a decaying brahmin colony in a Karnataka village, an allegory rich in realistic detail. Popular with critic and common reader alike since its publication in 1965, it was made into an award-winning, controversial film in 1970.

Samskara takes its title seriously. Hence, our epigraph is a dictionary entry on this important Sanskrit word with many meanings. (See the Afterword for a fuller discussion.)

I have tried to make the translation self-contained, faithful yet readable. But "the best in this kind are but shadows; and the worst are no worse, if imagination amend them."

A translator hopes not only to translate a text, but hopes (against all odds) to translate a non-native reader into a native one. The Notes and Afterword are part of that effort.

Many friends have willingly shared their expertise and good taste with me; I wish to thank the following especially:

Girish Karnad, who checked an early draft meticulously against the original and offered detailed suggestions; U. R. Ananthamurthy, the novelist, for permission and generous criticism; Philip Oldenburg, Donald Nelson, Edward Dimock and Molly Ramanujan at Chicago, Paul Engle, Peter Nazareth and others at Iowa for commenting on drafts and sections; Shirley Payne, who typed draft after draft, with tireless goodwill; *The Illustrated Weekly of India*, for serializing the novel in their columns; the editorial staff of the Oxford

University Press for reading all the proofs and for their friendship and patience.

A. K. RAMANUJAN
Chicago, 1976

SAMSKARA

In Memory of
M. G. Krishnamurti (1932–1975)